The Veggiecational Book

by Phil Vischer

Tommy NELSON™

Thomas Nelson, Inc.

Nashville

HOW MANY VEGGIES?

Art Direction: Ron Eddy

3D Illustrators: Thomas Danen, Robert Ellis, Aaron Hartline,
Adam Holmes, Mike Laubach, Joe McFadden,
Daniel López Mūnoz, Joe Sapulich, Ron Smith and Lena Spoke

Render Management: Jennifer Combs and Ken Greene

JUNIOR'S COLORS

Art Direction: Ron Eddy

Lead 3D Illustrator: Aaron Hartline

3D Illustrators: Thomas Danen, Robert Ellis, Joe McFadden,
Joe Sapulich and Nathan Tungseth

Render Management: Jennifer Combs and Ken Greene

PA GRAPE'S SHAPES

Art Direction: Ron Eddy

Lead 3D Illustrator: Aaron Hartline

3D Illustrators: Thomas Danen, Robert Ellis, Joe McFadden and
Joe Sapulich

Render Management: Jennifer Combs and Ken Greene

BOB AND LARRY'S ABC'S

Art Direction: Ron Eddy

Lead 3D Illustrator: Aaron Hartline

3D Illustrators: Thomas Danen, Robert Ellis, Mike Laubach,
Joe McFadden, Joe Sapulich and Nathan Tungseth

Render Management: Jennifer Combs and Ken Greene

Published in Nashville, Tennessee,
by Tommy Nelson,™ a division of
Thomas Nelson, Inc.

ISBN 0-8499-5865-2

Printed in the United States of America

98 99 00 01 02 WCV 9 8 7 6 5 4 3 2

Featuring these "Veggiecational" stories:

How Many Veggies?

Junior's Colors

Pa Grape's Shapes

Bob and Larry's ABC's

Dear Parent

We believe that children are a gift from God and that helping them learn and grow is nothing less than a divine privilege.

With that in mind, we hope these "Veggiecational" books provide years of rocking chair fun as they teach your kids fundamental concepts about the world God made.

– Phil Vischer
President
Big Idea Productions

How Many Veggies?

by Phil Vischer

Bob the Tomato is taking a trip.
A day on the sea will be fun!
How many veggies are on his small ship?

The answer, of course, is **1**!

Larry the Cucumber joins Captain Bob.
Could *he* find a place on the crew?
Maybe first mate — he'd be great for the job!

Now on the boat, there are **2**!

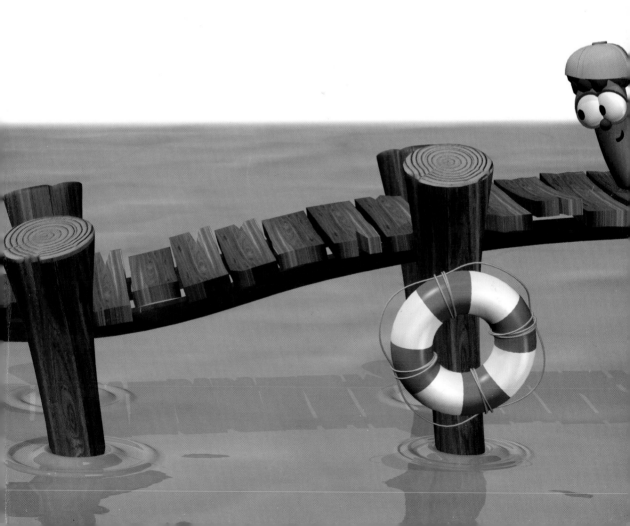

Two little veggies are taking a trip.
Junior says, "What about me?
I've got some crackers and soda to sip!"

Count them again, 1 – 2 – 3 !

Larry says, "Hey! Who will push us along?
I'm not very good with an oar.
Let's call Mr. Nezzer, because he's so strong!"

Now on the boat, there are **4**!

Junior says, "Captain! Our numbers are growing!
Soon we'll be rowing, the wind will be blowing,
But tell me please, how will we know where
    we're going
If no one is sitting up there?
We need someone up in the air!"

The gourd they call Jerry is next to arrive.
His compass and spyglass would help them survive!
So, quickly they vote him shipmate number 5!

And send him up high in the air —
To stare at the sea from his chair.

Five little veggies, no room for another,
The perfect vocational mix!
'Til Jerry says, "Boy, I sure do miss my brother."

And Jimmy becomes number **6**!

"Six is enough!" Bob remarks to his men,
"At least it's not ten or eleven."
But Percy jumps in, and when Bob counts again —

1 – 2 – 3 – 4 – 5 – 6 – **7** !

"Only one thing that we're missing!" says Larry,
"A parrot! Now that would be great!"
Then Laura shows up with her pet parrot, Harry.

And now on the boat there are !

Eight little veggies and one silly parrot
(Who came, you'll remember, with Laura the Carrot).
"The weight, sir!" says Junior, "our boat cannot bear it!
We're headed for trouble, I think —
Our boat is beginning to sink!"

Yes, eight little veggies, all trying to bail!
Starting to argue and whine —
"I'm coming!" yells Archie, "and I've got a pail!"

He jumps in, making it **9**!

Nine little veggies, all wet to their knees,
Beginning to shiver and shake,
Turn to see something come out of the trees
That makes their hearts quiver and quake!

Goliath the giant — a big, bumpy pickle —
Runs down to the dock with a shout!

"I'm no good at sailing, but I just love bailing!
So I'm going to help you guys out!"

10 little veggies, all taking a bath,
As soggy as soggy can be.
One little parrot looks back with a laugh
And pilots his boat out to sea!

Junior's Colors

by Phil Vischer

Junior Asparagus loves to draw.
He knows all his colors, too!

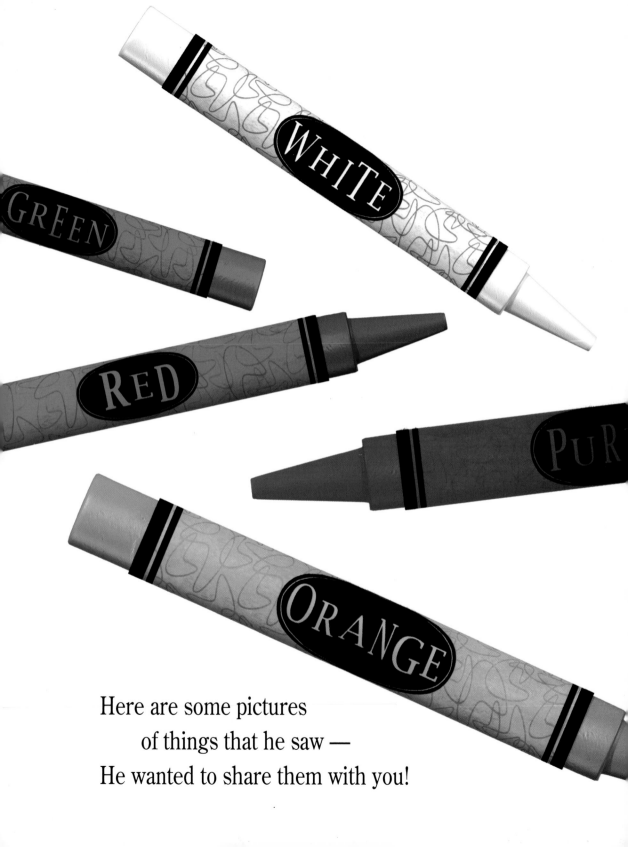

Here are some pictures
of things that he saw —
He wanted to share them with you!

White is the color of big fluffy clouds
That float through the sky overhead.

WHITE

A marshmallow's white,
and a big snowball fight,

But Bob is
very red.

ORANGE

Orange is the color
of Laura the Carrot
And Lenny and Jimmy Gourd, too.

Yellow is mellow.
It's great for your Jell-O!
Or maybe the fur on a cat —

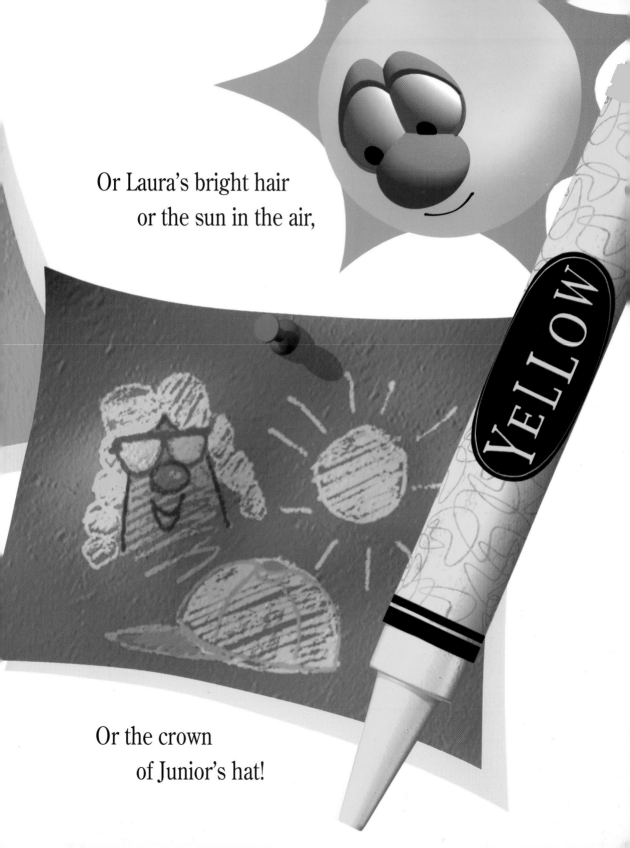

When Junior gets dirty
and needs a good scrub,
The water is
sparkling **Blue**.

So is the boat he
can float in his tub.

And the bottle that
holds his shampoo!

Black is the color
of nighttime —

BLACK

When Junior is
tucked in bed.

A bowling ball's black,
  and a licorice snack,

But Bob is very red.

Junior finds **Purple** on
lilacs and orchids,
The flowers his Mom
likes the most!

It's also in use
in his favorite juice

And the jelly
he puts
on his toast.

Green is the color
of springtime —

Of grass and
bushes and trees!

GREEN

That's why if you fall
when you're
chasing a ball
You get green on your
elbows and knees!

When God made the world,
    he used all sorts of colors —
Some of them brighter
    and some of them duller.

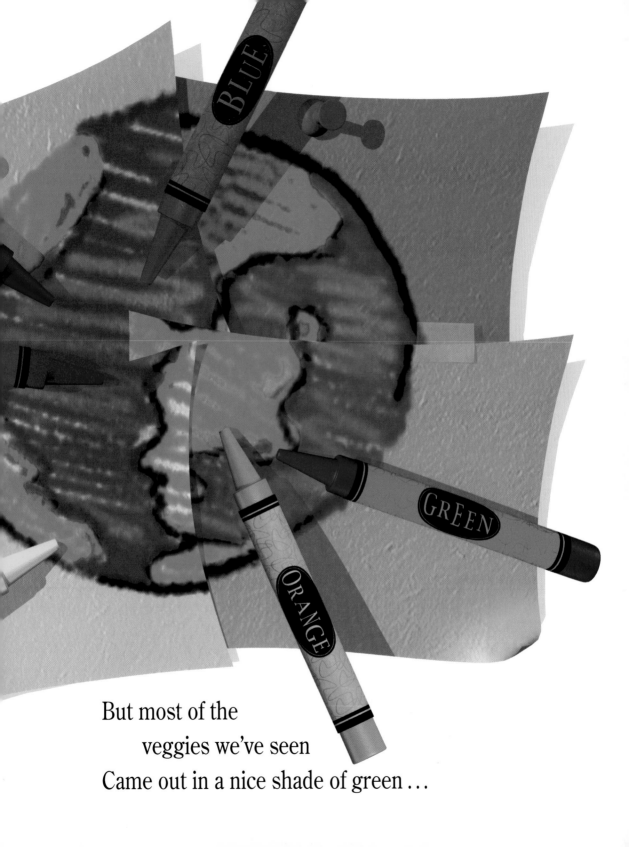

But most of the
veggies we've seen
Came out in a nice shade of green ...

To see what we mean,
look at Phil Winkelstein.

Or old buddy Larry
(but not Jim
and Jerry).

How 'bout Junior's mother?
Or Percy Pea's brother?

The scallions
(all three)
and Archie,
you see,

Are green
from toe
to head…

But Bob is very **Red**!

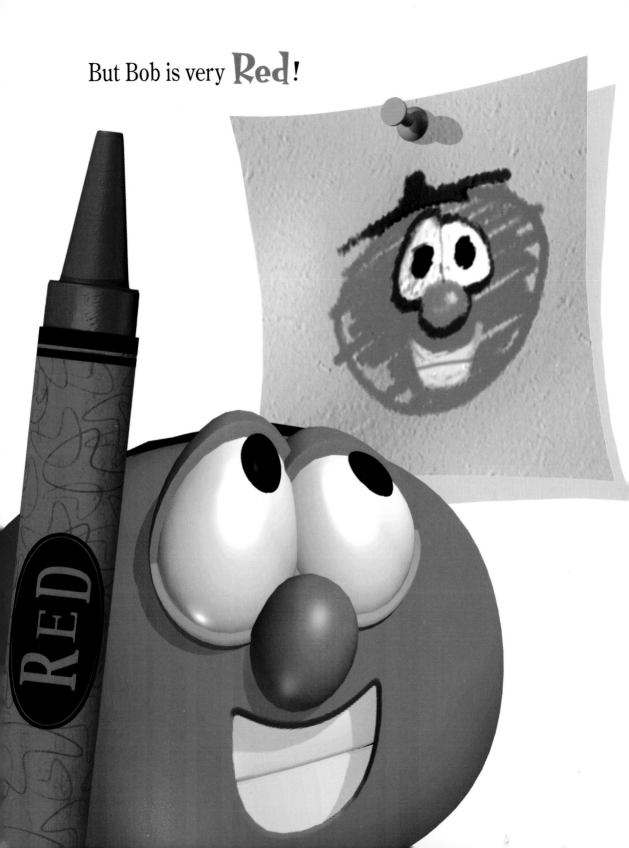

Pa Grape's Shapes

by Phil Vischer

This is Pa Grape. He loves the outdoors!
He loves what God made —
   all the mountains and shores!

He'd like to go visit the stuff he admires.
But look! His old car doesn't have any tires!

This is Pa Grape and the thing with the screen
Is his Robo 2000 New Tire Machine!

"It's really quite easy," says dear old Pa Grape.
"To get a new tire, just pick out a shape!"

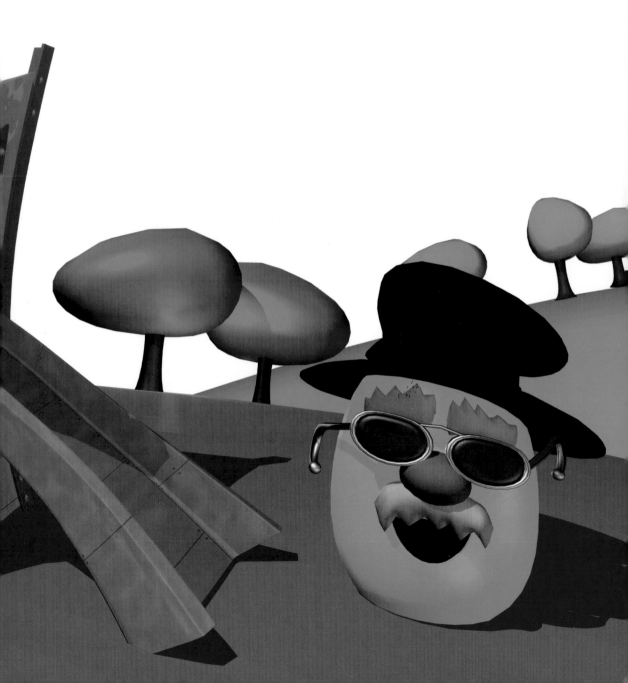

"But I can't remember — oh, dearie! Oh, me!
What shape does a tire for my car need to be?"

"Maybe a triangle! That ought to work!"
And the box springs to life with
a groan and a jerk —

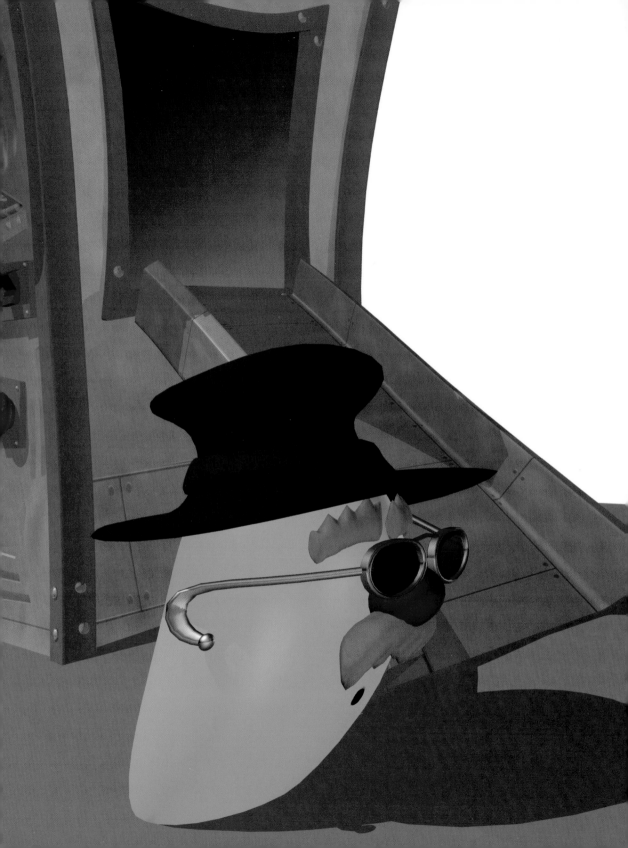

And spits out a tire not too big, not too small,
That just sits on the ground — without rolling at all.

"Oh, dear," says the grape. "That's not good,
    that's not good!
A tire should be rolling! I know that it should!"

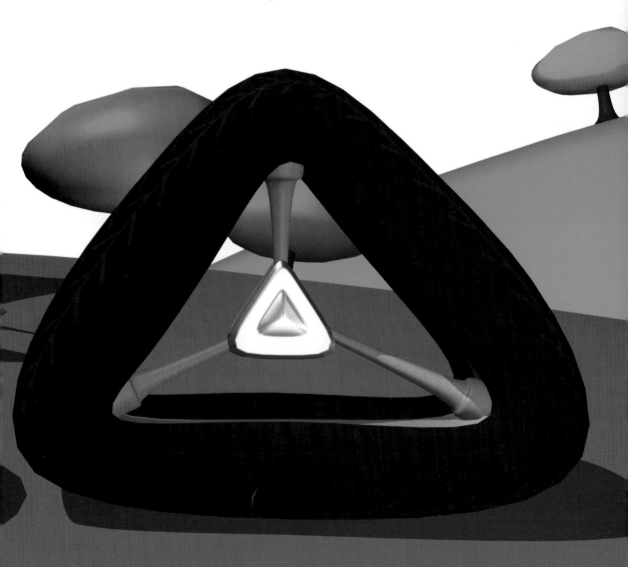

"Let's try a square! Oh, that's a nice shape!
I think it's just right for my car," says Pa Grape.

square

The square hits the ground
with a big, heavy thud.
But roll it does not. Pa yells out, "What a dud!"

"I'll try a rectangle, just to be fair."
But it doesn't roll any more than the square!

rectangle

"Here's an idea — I'd bet my new sweater!
Maybe a shape that is round will roll better!"

So Pa tries a crescent. "The back part is round!"

crescent

But once it rolls over, it sticks in the ground!

"Maybe an oval! It's round all the way!"

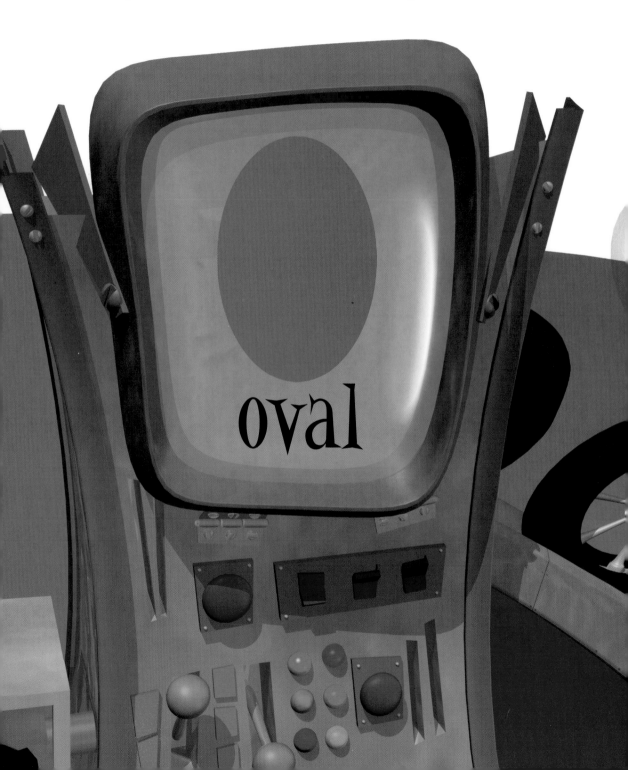

oval

And out pop four ovals.
"They're rolling! Hurray!

I guess if it rolls it just *might* do the trick —
But that wibblin' and wobblin' will make us all sick!"

Now, here is a circle. The very last shape.
"It looks quite a bit like a ball," says Pa Grape.

circle

"Hey! Balls are good rollers,
     I know that it's true!
So maybe a circle will roll nicely, too!"

At last, the new tire appears on the ramp.
It looks like a dream, and it rolls like a champ!

"It's perfect!" cries Pa. "Oh, so smooth and so round!
The tire for my car I have finally found!"

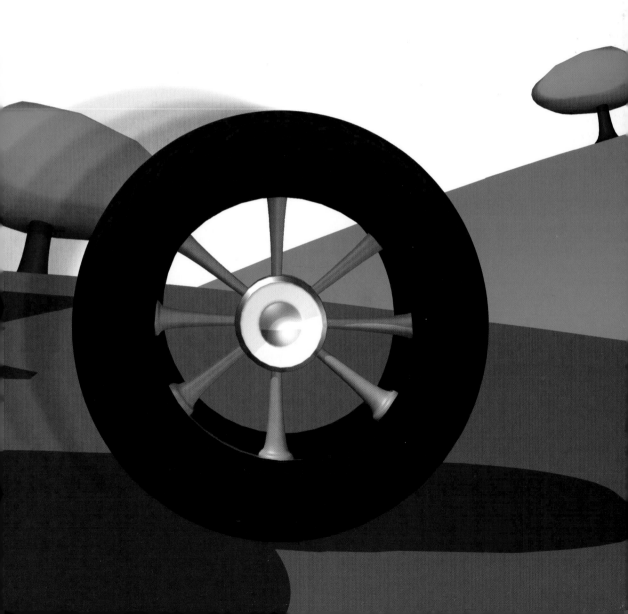

"Only one thing left to find now, I guess ...
I need a good friend to help clean up this mess!!"

Bob and Larry's ABC's

by Phil Vischer

If learning your letters is part of your job,
Meet Alphabet Larry
and Alphabet Bob!

A is for **Archibald.**
Look at his coat!

B is for **B**ob and his
big bamboo **b**oat!

C is for **c**ucumber
(this one's called Larry).
It's also for **c**arrots with
chocolate to **c**arry!

D is for **d**octor and **d**oorway and **D**ad.

E is for engine that makes Pa Grape sad!

F is for flowers from Flibber-o-loo ...

G is for George
and for
Grandma Grape, too!

H is for **hairbrush**. Oh, where could it be?

I is for island, far out in the sea!

J is for Junior! And Jimmy and Jerry ...
The very best buddies of Bobby & Larry!

K is for **k**ettle and **k**ing,
and you'll find
It also reminds us
to always be **k**ind.

L is for Laura ...

and **M** is for Mom.
She's **ma**king some **m**uffins
with Junior and Tom!

N is for **n**ecktie and
Nebby K. Nezzer …

is for **o**cean that hides sunken treasure!

P is for penguins and popular peas ...
A hero with plungers and singing palm trees!

Q is for **Q**werty, who
tells us the truth.

R is for **R**osie and dear old Aunt **R**uth!

S is for shepherd with **six silly sheep**
That need **standing** up
when they fall in a heap!

T is for toy box and bright, red tomato

U is for **u**nderwear
on a potato?

"**V** is for **veggies**!" says Alphabet Larry.
"We grow in the forest,
we grow on the prairie!

Wherever you find us,
in sand or in sod,
Remember we all were
made special by God!"

"But not just us veggies, as **W** knows,
God made the **w**hole **w**orld!
That's **w**hy everyone grows!"

Here is the end of the alphabet. See?
Just three little letters left ...

X, Y and **Z !**

"We need those three letters,"
says Larry, " to say ...
X-ray the **y**ellow
zucchini today!"

Alphabet Larry and Alphabet Bob!
It's time to go home now ...
         you've finished your job!

Go back to your rooms;
         feed your fish and your cats.
But please, first take off those ridiculous hats!